For Joe, thank you for inspiring me to dream big.
M. M.

For my mum, Melita Nyantakyi.
A. Q.

First published by HarperCollins *Children's Books* in 2022

HarperCollins *Children's Books* is a division of HarperCollins*Publishers* Ltd
1 London Bridge Street, London SE1 9GF

www.harpercollins.co.uk

HarperCollins*Publishers*
1st Floor, Watermarque Building, Ringsend Road, Dublin 4, Ireland

1 3 5 7 9 10 8 6 4 2

Text copyright © Manjeet Mann
Illustrations copyright © Amanda Quartey

ISBN: 978-0-00-850109-9

Printed in the UK

Small's
BIG
DREAM

Written by Manjeet Mann
Illustrated by Amanda Quartey

HarperCollins *Children's Boo*

Small lived in a *small* house.

She had a *small* room with
a *small* window and at night
she slept in a *small* bed with
a too-*small* blanket.

At school she wore small
shoes, which were too tight
for her small feet, and
a bag that was too
small for her books.

Despite being small,
Small had BIG dreams.

Every night,
Small looked
out of her
small window
at the giant city
that lay before her.

Small marvelled at the *tall* buildings.
She gazed at the *huge* park with its *tall* trees.
She beamed at the *never-ending* ocean.
She sighed in awe at the mountains that
disappeared into the stars.

Thinking about the **big** world made Small feel *even* smaller.

She had heard many times that those who live in small houses and sleep in small beds with too-small blankets and have too-small shoes on their feet *can't* have BIG dreams.

So Small hid her **BIG** DREAMS from everyone.

She kept them deep down
inside her, and if they
escaped she would

sit on them,

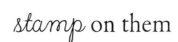

stamp on them

and *swallow* them back down.

But at night,
in her small bed,
snuggled in her
too-small blanket,
Small had BIG dreams.

She dreamed of *scaling* the
largest mountains,

sailing across
the oceans,

shooting off into **space.**

Small's dreams were becoming SO BIG
they were proving difficult to keep inside.

On the way to school, Small's dream started to GROW.

So she *sat* on it,

stamped on it

and *swallowed*
it back down.

But the dream just got BIGGER.

It **bubbled** out and
took Small with it, floating *up*, *up*, *up* towards the tops of the
tallest trees.

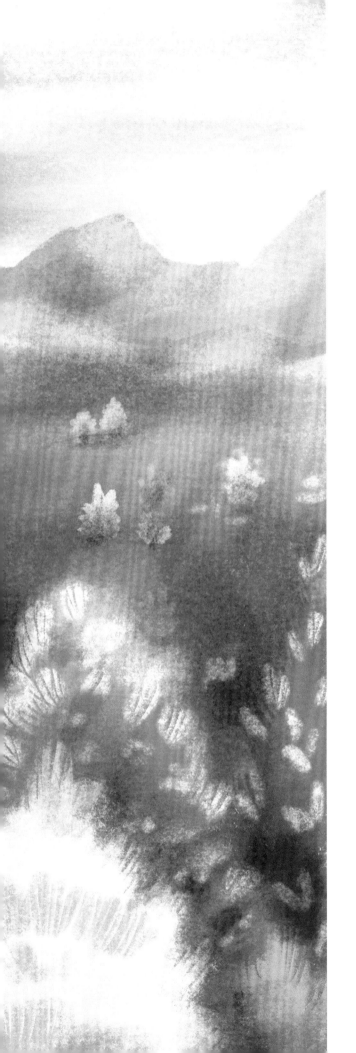

"Small!" shouted Mum.

"Small!" shouted the lollipop lady.
"Head down and feet on
the ground!"

So Small
climbed
down
from
the
tree.

On her way back from school, Small's dream started to
GROW once more and as much as she tried to
sit, stamp and *swallow* it away
    it **bubbled** out and took Small with it, floating *up,*

up
up,

towards the tops of the **tallest buildings.**

"Small!" shouted the teacher.

"Small!" shouted the caretaker.

"Head **down** and feet on the **ground!**"

So Small *stumbled* down from the building.

At night, Small sat in her *small* room
and stared out of her *small* window.

"Silly dreams," Small said in a small voice.

But before Small could
swallow it down, her
dream pulled her out
of the window and *up,*

up,

up

towards the **stars.**

Oh no! thought Small.
Head **down,** *feet on the* **ground!**

But her dream carried her
up, up, up until Small
landed on the **moon**.

Small looked out into **space**,
as far as her eyes could see, and saw
millions of other "Smalls" with
BIG dreams *floating* amongst the **stars!**

For the *first* time ever, Small BELIEVED in her BIG dreams.

Small saw that, no matter how *small* you might feel,
anyone can have **BIG dreams** and with the smallest
bit of courage you can make them come **true.**